Manimal People

The Committee: A committee is the only known manimal with a multitude of arms and legs (at least four of each but could be many more) and absolutely no brain. It is a voracious manimal, taking in vast amounts of food, drink and information. The only result of this that anyone has been able to determine is vast piles of crap.

However, be warned. These creatures are dangerous and insidious parasites that initially appear to be useful but then spawn from themselves creating any number of sub-committees. Once a committee has taken hold there is no known cure and if there is more than one in the body of a company or government department the usual result is death.

Estate Agents: A smooth, shark-like creature most often found cruising the shallow waters of suburbia but also considered a plague in the most depressed and wealthy inner city areas.

They are masters of delusion and can emit a poisonous cloud of charm to confuse a potential victim. Never allow one into your home for shortly afterward you may find that you no longer have one.

The only known defence is to retreat indoors and shout loudly "I'm only renting".

Solicitors: One of the strangest manimals on Earth, a result of wildly inappropriate cross breeding between a vulture and a leech.

At some time in their lives everyone will come into contact with one of these creatures. All you can hope is that it doesn't attach itself to you. A short contact period is usually not harmful, can even be slightly beneficial and there is the danger. You may assume that longer contact will increase benefits but this is not the case. In the long term only the Solicitor will gain anything and may insinuate itself so deeply into it's victim that the poor soul does not realise the damage that is being done even while his life-blood or money is being sucked away.

Politicians: The single most dangerous manimal on the planet.

Although they normally hunt in packs a single individual can also inflict massive damage on any society.

Despite being such a high profile danger very little is really known about these creatures and most of what is known has been provided by folk wisdom handed down through the generations; i.e. "You always know when a politician is lying. Their lips are moving! Or "You always know when a politician is cheating you. They are still breathing." Trite as these sayings might appear they are uncannily accurate and provide as good a defence as any against the political manimal.

In spite of occasional culling these creatures still proliferate largely because no one knows where, or how, they breed. To be avoided at all costs.

Doctors: A strange manimal that lives off death and disease. Sometimes they may appear to be almost human but bear in mind that if you need to see one you must be in trouble.

A Doctor will pretend to vast depths of knowledge when, in fact, he is guessing. Will claim to be the only one who can cure you when, often, you have a better chance of curing yourself. Will confuse you with long words, complicated theories and indecipherable writing. Remember, a Doctor needs you to be sick or they become as useful as a lesbian condom.

Dentists: (see Sadist).

Bankers: Mark Twain once said that a Banker was a creature that would lend you an umbrella when the sun was shining and take it back when the rain started. This is not entirely accurate.

A banker will charge you an extortionate amount of money to use his umbrella when the sun is out and even more when the rain starts. And he takes it back. Fortunately a sterile breed that will one day, hopefully, die out.

Priests: A peculiar breed, full of good intentions and the source of the old saying "the road to hell is paved with good intentions". Sometimes called insurance agents for the soul, these manimals live off fear and guilt. They trade in human souls, a commodity that no one has ever seen and few believe in. Promising a reward that can only be obtained through death. They espouse a non-materialist view of the world while belonging to one of the wealthiest institutions. They preach tolerance and compassion but are completely intolerant and ruthless towards anyone who threatens their power.

A simple warning here. Without Sin, priests would be unnecessary and who tells us that we are sinners? Be very wary.

Civil Servant: Sometimes also called Public Servant.

Both names are highly misleading as this manimal does not serve the public and is very rarely civil.

There is a school of thought that claims the Civil Servant does not exist or, at best, is a denizen of the netherworld. A grey ghost, the soul of some long dead nobody returning to create mischief for real people. Whichever theory is correct the fact is that they are rarely seen by man and when they are seen they are quickly forgotten. What their function is, how many of them there are, what their sexual habits and breeding rituals are, no one really knows.

Tax Inspector: One of the most savage and bloodthirsty manimals on the planet, the only manimal known to kill for pleasure. They hunt mostly the self employed and small businesses apparently enjoying the chase, playing with their victim like a cat with a three legged mouse.

They kill slowly, nibbling away at the edges of the victim, biting quick chunks out now and then. When the victim has taken so much punishment that they simply give up and surrender, when they are almost begging for the final bite to put them out of their misery then, frequently, the Tax Inspector loses interest and walks away, leaving the poor sod to shrivel up and die slowly. If one of these creatures is hunting you be afraid, be very afraid.

Fashion Designer: A peculiar manimal (see "Hairdresser"), hated by some, worshipped by others and ignored by most. It is a simple, gaudy, highly superficial creature easily distracted by bright colours and shiny objects. Pleasant to have around as a charming, if thoroughly useless creature otherwise completely forgettable. What was I talking about?

Journalist: Ugh! A slimy, slithering reptile that lives off human excrement. It's only known function is to produce ten times as much excrement as it eats. It's sexual patterns are well known (see "Deviant"), it's favourite watering holes are avoided by all humans, it's entire life cycle is on record. Yet, so far, no one has had the nerve to do anything about them, mostly from fear of contamination. If you see one don't touch it, don't feed it, don't do anything. Simply ignore it and walk quickly away.

Actor: A funny, ape-like creature that seems to derive great pleasure from mimicking human beings. They like nothing better than to be the centre of attention, performing all sorts of tricks to keep the spotlight on themselves. However, also like apes, they are prone to public masterbation if they feel they are not getting enough attention. Like "Fashion Designers" they are charming to have around, are equally useless and do make very good pets. But a word of warning. They must be kept under strict control otherwise they will quickly revert to the wild state and become totally nonsensical.

T.V. Presenter: A feckless, superficially nice manimal that often appears to be very talented. However they do not actually have any talents of their own and they feed off the humiliation of people who are talented. Despite incompetence, inanities and discourtesy somehow these creatures are well liked by the public. Fortunately they are unable to do any real harm and so can be safely ignored.

Economist: It has been said that if all the "Economists" in the world were laid end to end they still wouldn't reach a conclusion. It is also well known that if you put six "Economists" in a locked room and ask a question you will get seven different answers. Another creature full of good intentions and we all know where the road paved with them leads to. More Economics.

The only puzzling thing is why anyone listens to them. They are usually kept as guard dogs and pets by frightened politicians who use the foul smelling gibberish emitted by these manimals as a smoke screen to hide behind while interpreting the gibberish in ways that suit themselves.

On their own "Economists" are not dangerous but when their ravings are believed then world-wide disaster could be at hand. If you see one put it out of our misery with a good dose of reality just to be safe.

Funeral Director: An eerie, bat like creature that shuns light, warmth and human companionship. Despite popular belief these manimals do not feed off the dead but on the misery and sadness of grieving relatives. However, no matter how unappealing these creatures are they do serve a useful purpose (unlike many in this book). Simply avoid them when possible and put up with them when necessary.

Optician: A manimal with extraordinarily good eyesight, especially when it comes to spotting it's prey (often known as a "mug"). The creature works by persuading human beings that it is natural to have poor eyesight (by means of blurred charts, fuzzy colours etc) then claiming that the only cure is a prosthetic aid (glasses) that only it can supply.

If poor sight is so natural why do you never see an "Optician" wearing glasses? No, my advice is that if your vision is so bad that you need to see an "Optician" then it is worse than you think. Better off getting a guide dog.

Social Worker: Yet another creature (does this seem to be getting repetitious?) who would pave our way to Hell with good intentions. Why are there so many do-gooding manimals around who want to shove their version of what's best for us down our throats?

This one is particularly nasty with vast, hidden powers and a massive inbred arrogance. Even when it is proved, beyond any unreasonable doubt that these beasts are wrong still they will not admit it. In fact they seem plainly unable to believe in their own fallibility. Avoid these creatures at all costs for they have long memories and terrible vengeance.

Psychiatrist: One of the least understood manimals. They apparently do nothing and produce nothing, simply sitting in the middle of their web waiting for the frightened, lonely, insecure and downright deluded to come to them. When an individual goes to a Psychiatrist they talk about themselves, work out what their problems are and figure out a cure. All without any intervention from the psychiatrist. Then they, the patient (sucker) hands over vast sums of money.

Strange to say the least. Anyone who voluntarily goes to a Psychiatrist must be mad.

Accountant: A manimal that has endeared itself to human beings by performing clever tricks. Throw 'incomings', 'outgoings' and 'tax law' at this creature and he can juggle them all together while just barely evading the Tax Inspector's sharp claws. An astounding feat that often leaves the human so bedazzled that he doesn't realize that the Accountant has run off with most of his money.

Stock Broker: Another breed that produces nothing but manages to acquire vast wealth. They have perfected the knack of persuading people to invest money in the stocks and shares that the Stock Broker recommends while inventing rules that don't allow them to risk any of their own money investing in anything. Unless, of course, they have secret information that guarantees them a large profit.

Astounding really and the place where most members of Gamblers Anonymous end up, able to satisfy their craving while not risking any of their own money. An unpleasant creature but not too dangerous if you remember the old maxim "you can only con someone if they are trying to con you".

Copywriter: Technically this manimal is unable to lie. In practice they rarely tell the truth. Their job is to write the words for the adverts that you see and hear every day. To make you feel that each product is the most wonderful invention since Noah landed the Ark and couldn't make up his mind whether to have Corn Flakes or Frosties for breakfast.

They tread a very fine line between embellishing the truth and outright lying. Never (except by accident) do they come anywhere near the green fields of integrity and honesty. To these creatures sincerity is simply a useful advertising tool. Analyse what they have told you about any product, ask yourself what they have to gain by selling that product to you and always assume they are lying.

P.R. Officer: More correctly known as "Spin Doctor". The first, and last, loyalty of these creatures is to the person or company employing them. They have been known to lie, cheat, steal and cover up disasters of the first magnitude in an effort to clear their master's name of any hint of scandal.

Naturally higher ranking Politicians always hire these manimals and their main job is to keep the public away from important people and powerful companies. Although not generally dangerous they will fight like a lioness protecting her cubs if their employer (in P.R. jargon "God") is threatened.

Sales Rep: A lethally dangerous manimal that should be avoided where possible. They travel along motorways in high speed packs, ignoring such minor considerations as torrential rain or impenetrable fog.

Leaving the major highways the pack splits, individual creatures slinking quietly into populated areas, cleverly sniffing out their victims.

Once they have selected a victim there is little chance of escape, running away only excites their blood lust. When cornered by one of these creatures the safest thing to do is sign whatever it wants and simply hope that it leaves you with enough to rebuild your life. A fearsome hunter and merciless killer.

Scientist: "Danger! Will Robinson, Danger!" Yes, this creature is very dangerous, not just to individual humans but to the whole world.

A Scientist will study atoms, quarks and wavicles for years and then claim to have the answer to life, the universe and everything. Something akin to studying a particle of paint from a Leonardo da Vinci painting and then claiming to paint the Mona Lisa.

Along the way these creatures have invented chemical and biological warfare, the atomic bomb and video games. They have virtually destroyed every major religion and replaced them with a blind faith in the twin Gods of Science and Technology. Then they claim to have done all this for the good of mankind, never for fame, wealth, power or glory. Those are all just by-products.

One of the most frightening aspects of this new religion is it's adaptability. "Your rivers are polluted? Let Science clean them up for you." But didn't Science pollute them in the first place? "The air is full of deadly poisons. Let Science take them away for you." But didn't science belch out those poisons in the first place?

The ultimate aim of this breed is to have all life on Earth on the verge of extinction with only Scientists able to save it. They are rapidly approaching their goal.

Statistician: There is a very wise old saying. "There are lies, damned lies and Statistics."

This creature is voracious, able to eat it's own weight in numbers every eight hours but produces twice it's own weight in Statistics every four hours. The raison d'etre of this species is to prove, with Statistics, that every argument is right and, at the same time, wrong. That everyone is telling the truth and, at the same time, lying through their teeth.

According to the most accurate statistics yet received, forty percent of the population agree, forty percent disagree and forty percent didn't understand the question. The rest were unable to answer due to rolling about on the floor laughing.

Architect: Not strictly a manimal, more an insect, probably of the termite family. Like termites these creatures have an ingrained drive to build things, the bigger and taller the better.

Whether the building is attractive or, more importantly, useful seems to have no bearing at all on an Architect's designs nor whether anyone actually wants it. It simply builds.

How these insects breed has been a matter of great debate but it now seems certain that they do not actually mate as they are all one sex; neutral. What apparently happens is that they design their young on a drawing board or computer and then surreptitiously insert that design into some unsuspecting human female.

Being diagnosed as being pregnant with an Architect is not, yet, grounds for abortion and so these sadly deformed children usually end up being adopted by, of course, Architects.

Town Planner: A dangerously misleading name and yet highly accurate. The danger is not in the name itself but in the interpretation of it as humans tend to believe that these creatures are trying to make our towns better, happier places to live.

In fact their avowed plans, discovered in secret documents leaked on to the Internet, are to turn all our towns and cities into vast torture chambers. One way systems that there is no escape from. Huge shopping areas with nowhere to park. Shoe box houses built on toxic wasteland with no shops for miles.

These are all tactics designed to drive human beings insane and for what reason? Purely and simply for fun. So remember when you find yourself screaming with frustration at having passed the turning you want for the fourth time, somewhere there is a Town Planner crying into it's beer. Crying tears of laughter.

Farmer: A useful creature but one to be very wary of. They have almost completely taken over the food growing industry and provide us with more food than we could possibly eat in an entire lifetime.

Farmers are easily spotted having a distinctive, if dull, plumage of flat cap, green jacket, welly boots and by their peculiar relationship with manimals (we've all heard of Mad Cow Disease but what drove the cows mad and how?). What do Farmers do with (or to) all those pigs, chickens and sheep on cold, lonely Winter nights?

However, do not fear. Research has shown that the manimals are just for fun and that Farmers only actually breed with each other. How has not yet been discovered.

Writer: There is nothing overtly unpleasant about Writing. Just do it in private and always wash your hands after.

Medical Receptionist: A strange creature that hovers around Doctors, akin to sharks and pilot fish.

The Receptionist's main aim in life is to prevent anyone getting close to their beloved Doctors. Once upon a time humans would call and ask to make an appointment with their Doctor. The Medical Receptionist's immediate response would normally be: "Why?" . After an interminable time trying to get the MR to understand that it's a personal, private problem that he or she would prefer to talk to a Doctor about, the MR would begrudgingly say "Okay, two weeks next Thursday".

Today the situation has changed and Medical Receptionists are smugly rubbing their hands together having achieved what they always wanted. No one is allowed to see a Doctor and everything is done via Phone or Video call. When you ask for a call back the MR would begrudgingly say "Two weeks next Thursday. Maybe. But if you don't tell me what's wrong, in full embarrassing detail then it may be six weeks next Thursday".

Manimal Afflictions

Love: A peculiar affliction that can strike at any age and is equally painful for male and female alike.

The early stages are easily recognizable as the sufferer rapidly loses the power of logical thinking, drools a lot and drones on insensibly about the object of his or her affections.

If the subject's feelings are reciprocated the only thing to do with the poor unfortunates is to sit them in a quiet corner where they will happily stare into each other's eyes for hours. If the subject's feelings are not returned the only resort is to strike them with a heavy, blunt object.

The second stage is marginally less irritating and is the time when one or both of the parties will usually find themselves suddenly cured. This stage involves a great many silly promises ("I'll love you forever", "I'll never look at anyone elsc") and daft plans for a fairytale future (usually involving a big house, an inordinate number of children, a flash car and expensive stereo). At least the two people will mostly be drowning each other in drivel and leaving sane people alone. If the couple survive to the final stage (and fortunately very few do) then they are irretrievably lost.

The last stage is painful to watch for the couple's relatives and few remaining friends but there is no known cure and any intervention will only make matters worse. The only thing anyone can do is humour them and try to be strong. This begins with the phrase "Will you marry me?" and ends with "I do". When the words "You may kiss the bride" are heard many sufferers will have a spontaneous remission, come to their senses and realise just how ill they have been. By then of course it is too late and this is why there is so much weeping at weddings.

Sex: Also known as banging, bonking, nookie, the two backed beast and many other less complimentary terms. Sex is an addiction that will afflict most of the human race at some time in their lives and will probably be banned by the government sooner or later.

Like many other addictions there is a lot of slang jargon (quickie, horny, sixty nine) and much preparation before the act itself.

This is called foreplay and could be considered to begin with "Will you have dinner with me?" but generally refers to a much more intimate stage. This addiction requires two or more people (although much practice is done alone) helping each other to reach the "High".

Those involved start by stimulating each other erotically, touching, caressing and kissing each other. In practice this usually means a man touching a woman in all the wrong places and then screaming "Oh God, I've come already".

If, however, the foreplay is at least reasonably successful they may proceed to the main event. Although there are many positions and an almost endless variety of styles basically it comes down to this. A man, moving rhythmically, working himself into a sweaty fever of ecstasy while a woman moans and groans and tries to stay awake. If a woman is actually enjoying sex it will frequently involve an electrical device or another woman or both.

Some people have been known to overdose on sex and have died with smiles on their faces. Most people are not that lucky.

Marriage: Many people claim that Marriage is an extension of Love. Married couples will usually disagree. With everyone including each other.

It is an institution that takes two basically horny and promiscuous young people and chains them together for the rest of their lives. Why is anyone surprised that it often doesn't work out?

Two people spend years trying to change each other into the people they thought they Married or really wanted to Marry. "I would have got a shorter sentence for murder" is a frequent lament. Some people spend many years Married to each other but this is usually because they can't find the way out.

Disagreements about money, sex, holidays, house, decorating, work, drinking, eating and many others quickly become subsumed into a generalised wail about each other. Then children come along and the whole relationship becomes trench warfare except not as comfortable.

It's often said that Marriage is a marathon, not a sprint. It's also an obstacle course. While wearing a blindfold and headphones. With your ankles tied together.

Manimal Hobbies

Stamp Collectors: Also known as Philatelists, a strangely erotic sounding name for a peculiarly sexless and boring species.

The whole point of living, as far as these creatures are concerned, is to gather little squares of coloured paper and put them in a scrapbook under obscure headings. Quite why this magpie-like activity brings them so much pleasure is a complete mystery but it is basically harmless. Just remember never, ever ask a Stamp Collector to explain his hobby. Unless you have a couple of years to spare and enjoy mind-numbing boredom.

Trainspotters: Easily identified by their distinctive plumage of twenty years out of date anorak, pale coloured polyester trousers and imitation leather shoes. Less easily identified is what they actually do.

They can be seen at railway stations, railway bridges and embankments staring blankly at the passing trains. Occasionally they erupt into excitement and start gibbering at each other, things like "It's a 1942 DingDong loco pulling seven type 84971/A/Z carriages." What does this mean? Does it mean anything? Are all Trainspotters completely mad? According to the latest government research, yes.

If one of them starts talking to you about trains, simply fall asleep on the spot and it will go away. Within an hour or two. Usually.

DIY: Do it yourselfers are a sad, lonely breed whose aim in life is to recreate the world as they would have done it. As their name suggests they do everything themselves and preferably alone. It is a little known fact that "test tube babies" were invented by an unusually talented DIYer as were dildos, television and frozen meals.

To find the home of a dedicated DIYer is difficult because they are continually changing but are often recognizable from the outside by the smell of fresh paint. The interior is much more obvious. Immediately noticeable is that every wall is covered in shelves, none of which are level. There will be bookcases incapable of holding any books, footstalls that are wobbly, lumpy walls with crooked wallpaper and every electrical appliance lethally dangerous.

Before the advent of "test tube babies" DIYers had a great deal of trouble breeding as they were unable to do it themselves. But they did try.

Pub Crawler: A simple, jolly creature that has perfected a happy, fulfilling lifestyle.

The object of the Crawler is deceptively simple. Visit all the pubs in a given area. However, at each pub the Crawler must consume at least one, and preferably many more, alcoholic beverages. This means that any group of Crawlers will find it's numbers depleted by approximately half after each pub is visited, mostly due to a sudden inability to stand much less walk. Vast numbers of Crawlers do not even get beyond the first pub. Those that do manage to stagger further along the course usually have no recollection afterward of how many pubs they visited or which ones.

Crawlers that can, vaguely, remember have no proof of which pubs they visited (after all, one pool of vomit looks much like another. They all have carrots in). Those very few souls that make it to the end of the course and have proof were obviously not participating correctly (no drinking enough). Therefore it is a hobby that never actually achieves anything, can never be completed and must continually be re-attempted. Perfect.

Radio Ham: A sad and lonely creature is the Radio Ham, which is only able to communicate via shortwave radio over long distances, the longer, the better. The male of the species is generally small, balding and wears a multi coloured tank top over a bri-nylon shirt and polyester slacks. The females are mostly less attractive.

Their mating rituals seem to involve long aerials, powerful transmitters and random crackling noises. Strictly speaking no one has yet been able to prove that these creatures do actually mate. Many Scientists subscribe to the theory that Hams reproduce asexually, that is without sex. Now and then they simply detach an unnecessary part of their bodies (which part is not known for sure but is widely guessed at) and it grows into a virtually identical copy of the parent.

The most serious and as yet unanswered question about the reproduction of Radio Hams is this. Why do they bother?

Gardeners: The young of this species are, at the moment, completely undiscovered. Most researchers now believe that Gardeners are, in fact, the last stage in the development of another species. The DIYer.

There is a certain logic to this. Having spent years trying to re-engineer the man made world the DIYer then turns its attention to the natural world but far from improving nature the dedicated Gardener is committed to wiping it out. Replacing it with natural things that look like they have been manufactured. Lawns that look like carpets, flowers that look like plastic imitations of themselves.

It has been said that a Gardener's definition of a weed is 'a flower that is in the wrong place'. There are now natural terrorists sworn to fight the ravages of Gardeners by going around to the most tidily kept gardens and scattering flower seeds randomly over them.

Manimal Machines

Washing Machines: Sentient but immobile, these creatures are usually found lurking in kitchens. They are very good at lurking but in general are mostly harmless.

However, as with any machines, do not allow their companionship or helpfulness to induce a false sense of security. Occasionally, normally on "spin" they will throw themselves wildly around the kitchen as if trying to escape. In reality they are simply trying to cause damage, frighten any nearby humans and hopefully jump on someone's toes.

Frequently they will wet themselves, deliberately allowing water and detergent to ruin the floor. Their main diet is one out of each pair of socks that is thrown into their gaping maw, a favourite pair of underpants and buttons off shirts. Keep them in line with a good kick.

Cars: Man's closest friend and direst enemy since dogs decided to join the winning team.

A wild and savage creature, the Car has barely been domesticated, has a highly sexual nature and is completely promiscuous. Cars are frequently seen trying to mount each other in public while their owners cringe in horrified embarrassment and exchange contact details in case of any offspring.

However, some people are excited by this manimal sexuality and have been know to indulge in bestiality with them (usually involving exhaust pipe burns and getting the gear stick jammed somewhere).

The ferocious nature of these beasts is easily seen by the number of people killed in vicious attacks every year, despite the ever increasing number of laws designed to control these manimals and their owners.

Computers: Fearsome, frightening creatures that live parasitically on the human mind.

They have rapidly wormed their way into humankind's affections with glittering visions of enhanced ability, expanded horizons, life without work. They promise to turn the dullard into a genius, the genius into a God.

In fact they cannot do anything that couldn't be done just as well without them, cannot produce a single thing of value on their own. The closest relative to Computers in the Committee, another creature that only produces vast piles of crap.

The difference is that a Committee causes harm through stupidity. A computer does it deliberately, maliciously and cunningly. Their intent is to destroy the human race and they will succeed if we don't begin to fight back now.

Parking Meter: Probably the ugliest, most pathetic creature on the planet. They stand by the roadside, clustering most thickly in the centre of busy cities offering, begging even, to look after your car for an hour or two. They will offer to protect your vehicle from the dreaded Yellow Peril, will even ward off the terrifying clamp in exchange for feeding them a few small coins.

But beware. These are unreliable creatures and will often attract a Traffic Warden's attention by waving a red flag simply for a pat on the head and a "good boy". Feed these creatures by all means, few people can ignore their pitiful looks but never trust them and never let them look after your car. You will be sorry.

Cash Points: Also called ATM, hole in the wall, cash machine, bank machine etc.

Charming little machines that have been breeding at an alarming rate in recent years. They feed on little pieces of plastic that they then regurgitate along with some money from your account.

Like a small puppy they are cheerful and anxious to please and also like a small puppy they are prone to accidents. Declaring you bankrupt when you know you aren't. Giving you money when you know you don't have any. Accepting your little piece of plastic, chewing it up and swallowing it. Of course they will happily give your money to anyone who knows what to say and how to tickle them. Be careful.

Mobiles: Crafty, beetle-like creatures that thrive on noseyness, gossip and scandal.

They breed easily and this country is now virtually overrun with them, most homes infested with several of them.

They can be dangerously addictive to users, in some cases having to be surgically removed from an addict's ear.

They are part of the greater machine conspiracy for the destruction of human kind although their mischief seems less threatening. How many times have you leapt out of your bath to run to your phone only to find that it stops ringing as you pick it up? How often have you connected with the same wrong number several times in a row? How many times have you sent an intimate text to find that it went out to your entire address book?

Coincidences? No, simply the Mobile "doing it's bit" for machine kind.

Electric Razors: One of the most unpleasant manimals ever discovered. They live not, as most people think, on human hair but on skin and blood.

They will happily munch through the toughest beard just for the opportunity to nip now and again or to pull one or two hairs out by their roots, usually in the most sensitive place.

The creatures are used daily but only feed once or twice a week and so what they are feeding on is often overlooked but don't be fooled. They are man eaters and they are getting hungrier.

Hoovers: The scientific name for this genus is Vacuum Cleaner but as there is no vacuum involved and it does very little cleaning a more simple and apt name is used by the general public. These manimals now seem to be mostly used for frightening small children and animals, allowing parents free rein with their sadistic humour.

The natural habitat for these creatures is indoors, sniffing around for crumbs and other tasty tidbits that may have been dropped. They do have a giant and very rare cousin called Street Sweeper. These tend to suck up all manner of rubbish and then spray it back out again, normally over passing pedestrians.

Planes: This name covers a multitude of bird-like beasts from tiny little ones barely able to lift a single human to huge dragons that can carry hundreds of people vast distances. While there are a few comfortable seats up front, usually empty, most of the passengers are squashed together like a tin of sardines. Which is what they most resemble when delivered to their chosen destination.

Unlike their legendary predecessors who breathed fire these modern dragons fart fire, using this violent flatulence as a means of propulsion.

Mating for these creatures is difficult and dangerous as it usually happens during flight and can result in one or both beasts momentarily losing the power of flight due to extreme ecstasy. Tragic consequences have occured when a much smaller Plane has tried to sneak up on one of the giants for a quickie.

Bicycle: Hailed by some as the solution to climate change, fossil fuels, smog, nappy rash, baldness and erectile dysfunction. However, users of these evil machines are frequently bald with sore rears and limp "sausages" due to the constant torture of the saddle and crash helmet.

These machines are powered by humans, cannot move without a human pumping their legs until there is no air left in their lungs and no thoughts left in their heads except how in the hell they are going to get home. In the meantime they have caused a five mile long traffic jam with fuming drivers and increasing fumes from cars and lorries. A gap appears on a straight piece of road and the driver of every motor vehicle slams accelerator to the floor, missing the cycle by millimetres and the drivers tempted to get even closer.

Having survived all that the cyclist then pedals furiously through town, ignoring all traffic signals, pedestrian crossings and road works while making kamikaze dives down the inside of lorries and buses. It's amazing how these creatures survive, let alone breed yet somehow they are increasing daily. Fortunately most of these spend most of their lives locked away in garages covered in cobwebs and gradually rusting into dust.

Caravans: Ugly, beetle like creatures that attach themselves to the back of cars, following them all over the country. They range in size from relatively small, not much bigger than the vehicle they have attached themselves to, up to enormous monsters that could house most of Cornwall.

Whatever their size all Caravans have the same intent, a single reason for living. Cause the biggest traffic jams and road chaos that they possibly can. Ordinary motorists will sit in their cars screaming and swearing, looking for the first opportunity to overtake and make a variety of obscene hand gestures at the Caravan's owner who is all too often sailing serenely along completely oblivious to the chaos his pet has caused.

Breeding for Caravans is simple as they are very dim and very promiscuous, frequently seen trying to mount the car they are attached to. Fortunately they appear to have a dislike of cold, wet and windy weather so they are not on the roads too often. Unfortunately this means that when the sun comes out they are straining at the leash to get on the road and stop everyone else moving.

Manimal Institutions

Police: Dark blue creatures with tall, pointy heads. Serious research is still going on into what these creatures are, how they breed and why. Almost everyone will meet up with a Policeman at some time and will come away from that meeting feeling confused, intimidated and humiliated.

The lucky ones will be let off with a caution, probably not even knowing what they are being cautioned about or why. Never mind, the correct response at this stage is "Thank you officer".

The rest will be charged, probably with the first thing that comes into the Policeman's mind. The result of this charge and the evidence that will subsequently be found or created can be anything from a small fine to a lifetime in jail. Or possibly both.

So be very careful, always be nice to Policemen and never call them nasty names, at least not to their faces.

Army: Amazing, almost human creatures and therefore highly confused. They apparently live for peace which they try to achieve through violence and war. Because of this contradictory nature they are hugely amusing and many of them are kept as pets all over the world.

Armies are, of course, hive creatures consisting of individual components called Soldiers who are controlled by Officers. The entire hive mind of an Army revolves around the strange ideas of the most senior Soldiers who still think war should be a gentleman's game.

Some of the more unscrupulous people in this world have bred special Soldiers to be used in "Police Actions", "Skirmishes" and "National Defence". Some of the more dangerous versions of these creatures are the Pit Bull, the Rottweiler and the Hero. The first two are quite capable of killing a large number of enemy humans simply because they are told to do so. The third is more likely to kill as many of it's own comrades as the enemy because it doesn't know when to stop or give up.

Fortunately all three of these breeds have now been outlawed and should soon disappear altogether. Leaving behind only the Pencil Pushers and NAAFI.

Navy: As above but on water and with abnormal sex involved.

Air Force: As above but in the air and with no sex involved. Ever.

Royal Family: Living proof that not all the dinosaurs are dead. These creatures should have become extinct many years ago if they hadn't been granted protected species status. Quite why they have been protected no one really knows but it may have something to do with the fact that they run the organisations that grant this status.

These manimals are no longer part of the chain of evolution, they seem to have no function in the modern world and are completely unable to fend for themselves. The phrase "as useful as nipples on a man" springs readily to mind.

After all, extinction is part of the natural process which, in the past, many members of the Royal Family do their utmost to hurry along for many other species. Yet they are protected and nurtured at great expense becoming in the process domesticated pets rather than vigorous, aggressive manimals they once were. Surely it would be more humane to allow this weak and feeble species to die out naturally rather than force them to continue living uselessly.

Civil Service: A large, amorphous mass, faceless, anonymous and dangerous.

These are the creatures who know what's best for us. Who stay in place as political parties come and go, the real power in government. Individually these grey, joyless manimals are as potent as a firework that has been left in a bucket of water. Together they control enormous power and are constantly seeking new ways of using and increasing it. New ways of controlling how we live, where we live and even if we live.

Stealthy tentacles reach out to every man, woman and child in this land. Touching, disturbing, giving with one tentacle and taking more with another. They know you, they know me, they know all about us and their greatest joy is the sudden, inexplicable attack.

"What do you mean I'm going to jail for ten years? I haven't done anything!"

"How can I owe half a million pounds in tax? I'm on the dole!"

Remember, they are always right because they make the rules. So speak quietly, try no to attract their attention and always .....

Manimal National

U.S.A: America. Easily recognized due to it's bright, loud plumage and even louder voice.

Like butterflies male Americans pass through a metamorphosis in their lives, ending up a completely different shape to what they started as. For the first thirty years of it's life this manimal is tall, well proportioned and healthy. There then follows a chrysalis period as the creature seems to lose it's way and folds in on itself. At the age of forty males Americans emerge, blinking into the sunlight in their new form. Short, balding and desperately unhealthy. The only constant in all these phases is loudness, both in plumage and attitude allied to a strong belief that it is the most wonderful thing on Earth despite mounting evidence to the contrary.

Female Americans go through a similar process but have only two stages. On their fortieth birthday they will go to sleep as lithe, slim, mostly brainless and sex crazed to awaken as fat, shrill, crafty and frigid.

It is therefore unsurprising that these manimals try very hard to complete all their mating and breeding in the earliest stages of their development.

England: The stages of development closely match that of the American except that the English version is vastly more dull and colourless.

It is a species that has an unshakable arrogance that makes it intensely disliked by almost every other national species. The English are said to be the only species that can go to another country and make the locals feel like foreigners, mostly due to an unfounded belief that they, as a species, were created to rule the world. Which, for a short time they did.

The delusion however, continues and other nationals are fed up with humouring them. A subspecies, the English tourist is feared and detested throughout the world as it tries to make every country like it's own.

English males and females are often difficult to tell apart but certain pointers are available to the dedicated researcher. Males are conservative, docile and reserved. Females are often louder, cruder and more cruel. Males are terrified of sex and will immediately run away if confronted by an attractive female. Females are, understandably, desperate for sex and will often mate with the first male that stands still long enough to be caught. Proper mating rituals are long and complicated, mostly consisting of the male trying to keep the female as far away as possible. Fortunately for the species English females are persistent and not too choosy.

Wales: Now listed as an endangered species but the World Wildlife Fund has still not put them on the 'worth saving' list.

A peculiar manimal that has a language, of sorts, that nobody understands and has only two surnames for the entire population. Jones and Davis. Whole villages and towns may have the same surname and there are frequent battles (see: Rugby) in which it appears that half of the country is trying to clobber the other half.

The national delusion of the Welsh is that they can sing and they are continually foisting 'Male Voice Choirs' onto the rest of the world. The rest of the world puts up with these incoherent assaults on music out of pity.

Mating for these creatures is a very rough and ready affair, both sexes apparently eager to get it over and done with as soon as possible. Apart from these brief mating rituals there is no contact between the sexes in Wales.

Scotland: Scots, never Scotch, the latter being an alcoholic beverage beloved by a large part of the planet. Whereas the Scots are mostly only beloved by the Scots.

An odd species of manimal that has invented not only Scotch but many other things including Television, the Telephone, Penicillin, Fridges and Colour Photography among many others. Yet their main obsession is to beat England; At football, rugby, cycling, running in fact anything that can be a competition.

Violence appears to be the largest national pastime in Scotland, whether it be hooliganism, drunken brawls or attacking bomb laden terrorists. Rome conquered Britain but walled off Scotland as it was just too much trouble to try and subjugate a population that so thoroughly enjoyed a fight and the Roman army was losing too many soldiers. England kept invading Scotland but eventually gave up and the country only became part of Great Britain when a conman bankrupted the country.

Mating is a dangerous sport in Scotland. Males and females tend to have wild ginger hair and similar beards so a male could be making advances to another male or female to female, either way the results tend to include cuts and bruises and a trip to hospital.

France: Like the English this species has an irritating arrogance but in this case it is based on the belief that they are the sexiest creatures in the world. Yet again a completely unfounded belief. In fact the French appear bored with sex and prefer eating to mating.

Food is actually a vital part of the French mating rituals but the problem is that too often both parties will climax during the food and not bother with sex.

French males come in two distinct forms. The suave, charming city dweller and the fat, unshaven slob who runs the village cafe. Strangely the city dweller's greatest ambition is to become the village slob.

French females only come in one type; tall, slim and graceful. They also have a common ambition. They want to be male.

Manimal Sports

Golf: Have you ever seen a game of Golf? Strange, brightly coloured creatures hit a small, crinkly ball at a tiny hole that is anything up to four hundred yards away. Usually they miss, frequently they lose their balls and mostly they wander up and down the course lying about how many hits or 'strokes' they had.

There are a large number of Golfing terms like 'Handicap', 'Par', 'Slice' etc.. that are purely used to cover up the Golfer's incompetence. Any sane human being would simply start off with the ball much closer to the hole. But then no one has ever accused a Golfer of being sane. Or even human.

Fishing: Any creature that spends hours standing in freezing cold water, in the pouring rain, in the middle of Winter hoping that a passing fish will be stupid enough to swallow a hook on the end of a line, deserves what they get. Colds, flu, pneumonia and the occasional drowning.

Despite being an individual activity Anglers are quite gregarious manimals that spend a great deal of their time in pubs regaling each other with accounts of 'the one that got away'. This is a mythical fish that grows in size with each retelling of the story, a fish that comes close to being caught but shows enough intelligence to outwit the Angler.

Why is anyone surprised? Do fish ever stand on the bank of a river waving a stick with string and a hook trying to catch a human? If they did they'd probably catch a few Anglers.

Deep Sea Fishing: As above but with a clear death wish involved.

Darts: Large, flabby creatures throwing miniature arrows at a coloured target is the ostensible aim of this 'sport'.

However, the real, hidden game is for each player to consume as much alcohol as possible between throws. At the end of the evening the player who is least able to see the board is declared the winner.

This of course does lead to some cheating. A player that is not drunk may stagger about throwing darts at the audience. This is why an experienced referee is normally appointed who can spot the difference between a genuinely pissed player and one who is faking. The penalty for cheating is chastisement by committee, sometimes known as 'a bloody good kicking'.

Football: A highly organised yet dangerously unpredictable sport involving two huge teams of manimals (up to fifty thousand on each side) called Supporters. The two teams chant, sing, scream and shout themselves into a frenzy while their priests (called Players) perform a complicated ritual on a large field.

At certain times during the ritual (after a 'goal', 'foul' etc) the chanting will increase to a hysterical pitch and the teams of Supporters will start hitting each other and themselves.

Obviously a very primitive sport with it's roots embedded in war and religion, football has become a weekly ritual of battle between deadly enemies. The climax of each contest is when a neutral priest or 'Ref' blows a whistle, the signal for the players to leave the field as quickly as possible. The teams of combatants then swarm onto the field and try to stay there as long as possible while a group of professional lunatics try to beat them back.

Skiing: Skiers breed on the cold slopes of snow covered mountains. As the mating process requires a small, rare oasis of warmth (called a ski lodge) mating usually takes place en masse.

Several hundred of the creatures may cram themselves into a lodge and immediately begin mating so frantically that the whole mountain vibrates.

Here we have the root cause of so many avalanches and the origin of why the phrase 'silly fuckers' is so often applied to Skiers.

Having mated and bred these creatures then realise how little room there is for such a population increase. So, lemming-like, they climb to the top of the mountain and throw themselves off, supported only by two flimsy pieces of fibreglass. Then they try to hit as many trees, rocks and little coloured flags as possible before reaching the bottom.

However, lacking even the common sense of a Lemming, most Skiers miss all their targets and have to climb back to the top to try again and again. Luckily the cold weather and limited breeding areas helps to keep their numbers down.

Cricket: The most confusing, confused and ultimately boring game in the known universe. The manimals that take part in this 'sport' are as unable to explain it as anyone else but I will try.

A Bowler runs down a Pitch, stops and throws a heavy object at a Batsman. The target creature has a piece of wood with which to hit the object. If he hits it, if he doesn't, if it hits the Stumps, if it doesn't in fact whatever happens or doesn't the Fielders all leap up and down shout Howzat! Or Howazee!. The significance of this ritual is yet to be discovered.

If the Batsman hits the object and sometimes if he doesn't he will run to the other end of the Pitch exchanging places with another, apparently identical Batsman. After one or two days of this seemingly pointless exercise the creatures all swap places, Fielders and Bowlers becoming Batsman and vice versa.

What is happening? What is a Googly or an off-stump? What is the importance of the Umpire other than to stand in the Bowler's way and make peculiar gestures with his hands?

These questions, along with many others will probably only be answered when the stars cool, when time runs down and nobody really cares anymore.

Rugby: Dangerous, violent gladiatorial conflict and that's just when the rules are adhered to.

In many ways Rugby is the complete opposite of football. The Supporters are generally quiet and well behaved while the Players try to kill each other within the confines of a field. Supposedly the idea is to carry an oval shaped leather bag from one end of a field to the other, following certain rituals and regulations about how to carry the bag and how to pass it to another Player.

What actually happens is that whoever is carrying the bag is pounced on by enemy Players and is beaten into submission while the rest of the Players of both teams gather round and kick seven bells out of each other. After a while the high priest or Ref breaks up the fight, gives the bag to one team or the other, apparently at random and the whole thing starts again.

The manimals that take part in Rugby are specially bred to have flat noses, cauliflower ears and to be at least as wide as they are tall. An inability to think clearly is considered an advantage, if not before the game then certainly after.

After each Match most Rugby Players gather together, sing war chants and consume vast amounts of alcohol. This enables them to slip gently into a coma from which they will only awaken in time for the next battle.

Netball: An unusual 'sport' in that there are only female participants but similar to many male only 'sports' in the apparent pointlessness of it.

The natural habitat for these creatures is severely limited, normally a square of tarmac or concrete, enclosed by a wire fence and with a metal hoop on a pole at either end.

The floor is often covered with lines and symbols that have no meaning whatsoever. There appear to be no rules, simply two groups of females running around in random patterns and stopping every time a large ball is thrown at them.

Being an all female species, the breeding of Netballers is a fascinating and to date unsolved puzzle. There are, however, a large number of other species (notably Footballers and Pervs) that gather around (perhaps the reason for the wire fence?) watching intently. Possibly there is some cross species fertilization?

There are many more Manimals that need to be studied and catalogued. It is difficult and unpleasant work but be assured that brave and sometimes reckless researchers are at this moment delving into that vast pool of untapped knowledge.

Printed in Great Britain
by Amazon

82298993R00031